Cenchild

ABY6846

SANTA CRUZ CITY-COUNTY LIBRARY SYSTEM
0000107744633

D0467998

JEASY   Johnson, Angela.
            One of three
JOH

SANTA CRUZ PUBLIC LIBRARY

SANTA CRUZ, CALIFORNIA 95060

One of Three

by ANGELA JOHNSON
pictures by DAVID SOMAN

ORCHARD BOOKS   NEW YORK

SANTA CRUZ PUBLIC LIBRARY
SANTA CRUZ, CALIFORNIA

Text copyright © 1991 by Angela Johnson
Illustrations copyright © 1991 by David Soman
All rights reserved. No part of this book may be reproduced or transmitted in any
form or by any means, electronic or mechanical, including photocopying, recording
or by any information storage or retrieval system, without permission in writing
from the Publisher.

Orchard Books, A division of Franklin Watts, Inc.
387 Park Avenue South, New York, NY 10016

Manufactured in the United States of America.
Printed by General Offset Company, Inc.
Bound by Horowitz/Rae. Book design by Mina Greenstein.
The text of this book is set in 16 point Monticello.
The illustrations are watercolor paintings reproduced in full color.
10   9   8   7   6   5   4   3   2   1

Library of Congress Cataloging-in-Publication Data
Johnson, Angela. One of three / by Angela Johnson ;
pictures by David Soman.   p.   cm.
Summary: A series of candid reflections by the youngest of three sisters on her daily
relationships with her older sisters and family.
ISBN 0-531-05955-3.   ISBN 0-531-08555-4 (lib. bdg.)
[1. Sisters—Fiction.   2. Family life—Fiction.]   I. Soman, David, ill.   II. Title.
PZ7.J629On   1991   [E]—dc20   90-29316

To my beloved grandmother,
the late Mattie Werren Johnson
—A.J.

For Liana
sister, painter, and best friend
—D.S.

Since I can remember I've been one of three.
Eva, Nikki, and me.

One of three sisters that walk to school together.
Down the street together.
One of the three in the sun and the rain.

I'm one of the three that lives in apartment number 2,
has long hair and brown eyes, and can sometimes
play hopscotch by the trash cans
if I ask for a long time.

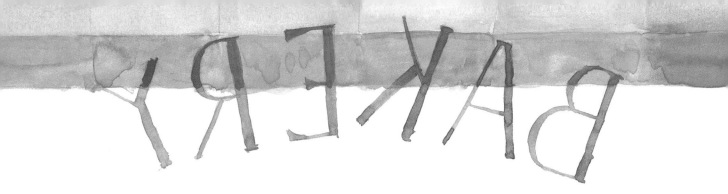

On Saturdays I'm one of the three that sits
outside the bakery and looks and smells and smells....

I'm one of the three that squeezes into the taxi
on snowy days with Mama, Aunt Sara, and Grandma,
and it's warm there.

I'm one of the three that looks just like our mama,
smiles just like our daddy,
and holds hands with my sisters in the store,
looking like triplets—almost.

I'm one of the three that likes the subway,
the people on it,
and the way our feet hang over the seats.

I'm one of three who lives over the flower shop.
Mr. Lowen still gets all of our names wrong,
but he gives us each a daisy every time.

We walk down the street like stairsteps,
and I'm in front.

Sometimes Eva and Nikki say I'm not invited to go with them. Not to the park, the store, or sometimes even for a walk.

I'm left behind.
Not one of three, just one.

Then Mama calls me Sister and says I'm too little
to go there or do that,
so maybe I just want to help her paint or read to her.

Daddy says that I have to be the baby sometimes,
and keep Mama and him company,
just sometimes.

I miss Eva and Nikki and me....
But when it's just Mama, Daddy, and me,
it's a different kind of three,
and that's fine too....

0000107744633